Magic Kitten

A Shimmering Splash

To Biff, the toothless tabby with issues.

GROSSET & DUNLAP
Published by the Penguin Group
Penguin Group (USA) LLC, 375 Hudson Street, New York, New York 10014, USA

USA | Canada | UK | Ireland | Australia | New Zealand | India | South Africa | China

penguin.com
A Penguin Random House Company

Text copyright © 2007 by Sue Bentley. Illustrations copyright © 2007 by Angela Swan. Cover illustration copyright © 2007 by Andrew Farley. All rights reserved. First printed in Great Britain in 2007 by Penguin Books Ltd. First published in the United States in 2014 by Grosset & Dunlap, a division of Penguin Young Readers Group, 345 Hudson Street, New York, New York 10014. GROSSET & DUNLAP is a trademark of Penguin Group (USA) LLC. Printed in the U.S.A.

Library of Congress Cataloging-in-Publication Data is available.

ISBN 978-0-448-46789-4   10 9 8 7 6 5 4 3 2 1

A Shimmering Splash

SUE BENTLEY

Illustrated by Angela Swan

Grosset & Dunlap
An Imprint of Penguin Group (USA) LLC

★ Prologue ★

The young white lion dipped his head toward the pool and drank deeply. It felt good to taste the water of his home again. Perhaps this time it would be safe to stay.

Suddenly, across the pool, a huge black adult lion emerged from some trees and leaped up onto the rocks.

"Ebony!" Flame gasped, as he looked

up at the terrifying sight of his uncle.

He felt sparks crackling in his fur, and there was a bright white flash. Where the majestic young white lion had stood now crouched a tiny fluffy amber-and-white kitten with a big amber patch over one eye.

Flame's furry kitten tummy brushed the ground as he edged slowly backward into the shelter of some tall rushes. As he lay there trembling with fear, hoping desperately that he had hidden in time, the rushes parted and a large dark shape came toward him.

Flame's tiny heart missed a beat. This was it! Ebony had found him!

"Prince Flame," rumbled a deep gentle voice. "I am glad to see you, but it is not yet safe for you to return."

Flame blinked at the adult gray lion in relief. "Cirrus. It is good to see you again. Tell me, how is my uncle ruling the kingdom he stole from me?"

Cirrus showed worn teeth as his lip curled with anger. "Ebony is strong and cruel and will never change. He is determined to find you and kill you so that he can rule forever."

"I am ready to face him now and take back my throne!" Flame mewed, his emerald eyes flashing with anger.

Cirrus nodded approvingly and reached out an enormous gray paw to draw the tiny kitten closer. "Bravely said, but you must first grow strong and wise. Use this disguise and go back to hide in the other world, where you will be safe."

"Nowhere is safe from my uncle's spies!" Flame answered.

As if in reply, another terrifying roar rang out. "I sense my nephew! Where are you, Flame? Show yourself!" growled an icy voice.

"Ebony knows you're close. Go now, Flame," Cirrus urged. "Save yourself!"

The tiny amber-and-white kitten whined as he felt the power building inside him. His fluffy fur ignited with sparks, and there was another bright flash.

Flame felt himself falling. Falling . . .

Chapter
ONE

Lorna Edwards caught her breath with excitement as the car drove off the ferry. In front of her, there was a wild landscape of mountains, lakes, and vast open spaces. Fluffy white clouds floated in the clear blue sky.

"Craggen is so gorgeous. I really love being back here!" she exclaimed.

"Me too," Flora Edwards said, turning

her head to smile at her daughter. "I expect you're dying to catch up with Ruth and Callum."

Lorna nodded. "I can't wait." It had been almost a year since she'd seen her cousins, who lived on the island off the north coast of Scotland. Now she was going to spend the whole summer vacation with them.

"You won't have to wait long. Marie and Hugh and the kids always come to meet us," Lorna's mom reminded her.

Lorna leaned forward, pushing back a strand of her short red hair as she peered out at the single-lane road. Just inland, the meadows were dotted with huge gray stones and patches of yellow grass. Lorna suddenly caught sight of some familiar figures, standing next to a parked car. "There they are!" she cried, bouncing up and down in her seat with excitement.

She could see Aunt Marie, Uncle Hugh, and Ruth, but Callum didn't seem to be with them. The minute their car stopped, Lorna opened the door and flew across to her aunt, uncle, and cousin. Everyone began speaking at once, and there were hugs all around.

"Lorna! You've grown tall since last we saw you," Uncle Hugh boomed. He was tall, with broad shoulders and dark hair, and he towered over his tiny wife.

"So you have," Aunt Marie agreed in her soft voice, pushing back a strand of curly red hair. "I expect you'll notice the difference in Ruth, too."

"Hi!" Lorna grinned at Ruth and gave her cousin a hug. At nine years old, Ruth was a year younger than Lorna. She had dark hair, like her dad, and her mom's sunny smile.

"Why do adults always talk about how much you've grown?" Ruth whispered, making a face.

"I know," Lorna said, giggling.

"What do they expect us to do, shrink or something?" She glanced at the car, expecting the back door to open any minute. It was just like Callum to hide inside and then jump out! But the car was empty. "Okay, I give up! Where's Callum hiding?" she said, grinning.

Ruth's face seemed to cloud over. "He didn't come. He went to a friend's house to do some homework. He said he'd see you at the farmhouse later."

"Oh," Lorna said, trying hard not to feel disappointed that her favorite cousin had chosen to do something else instead of coming to meet her.

"Shall we go?" Aunt Marie suggested. "I expect you'd like to relax over a cup of tea and a bite to eat after your long journey."

"Can I go in Aunt Marie's car?"
Lorna asked her parents.

"Of course you can, dear. I expect
you and Ruth have a lot of catching up
to do," her dad replied.

"Here, let me give you both a
hand!" Uncle Hugh said, with a gleam
in his eye.

"Uh-oh!" Remembering her
uncle's silly sense of humor, Lorna
attempted to dart out of his reach, but
she was too late. Hugh swept her up
and tucked her under one arm and
then did the same to Ruth. Marching
over to the car, he piled them both
into the backseat, where they collapsed
together, laughing breathlessly.

Lorna's parents laughed, too. Aunt

Marie shook her head. "I don't think Hugh will ever grow up!" she said with a fond sigh.

Lorna linked arms with Ruth in the back, as they drove toward the farmhouse. It was good to be back on Craggen, but it did feel strange not having Callum there, too.

"Thanks, Aunt Marie. That was yummy," Lorna said as she finished the last mouthful of delicious homemade cake. She and Ruth were sitting on the battered sofa in the comfy farmhouse kitchen.

Lorna's parents and her aunt and uncle were seated at the table. "Why don't you show Lorna my new workroom, Ruth?" Aunt Marie

suggested, as she passed her husband a
second huge slice of cake.

"Do you want to see it?" Ruth asked,
looking across at Lorna.

"Okay," Lorna said. It had to be better
than listening to the grown-ups gossiping.
She followed her cousin outside, and
they went across the yard to some stone
outbuildings.

"This is it," Ruth said.

"It's, um . . . very nice," Lorna said,

being polite. She peeped through the
workroom window. She could see
the big loom her aunt used to weave
blankets and throws from their own
sheep. Colorful balls of the wool,
which she dyed herself, were heaped
in baskets.

Ruth elbowed her in the ribs.
"Yeah, but weaving and stuff is totally
boring. Why don't you come and see
Mom's new sheep?"

Lorna grinned. This was more like
it! She loved animals, and her aunt and
uncle kept all kinds of unusual sheep.

Ruth stopped beside a pen and
pointed at six small sheep with dainty
black-and-white faces and crinkly
wool.

"Wow! They're beautiful," Lorna

said. "What kind are they?"

Before Ruth could answer, a moody voice cut in. "Who cares? They're just stupid sheep!"

"Callum!" Lorna felt a big grin stretching across her face as she turned around. "You're back!"

"Looks like it, doesn't it?" Callum muttered. He had his hands thrust into his jeans pockets, and his dark hair flopped forward onto his forehead.

Lorna's smile wavered a little. "It's really great to be here," she said anyway, hoping to encourage Callum to be a little more friendly.

"Whatever!" He shrugged. "I'm going inside. I'm hungry."

"Okay. See you . . . er . . . later,"

Lorna stammered.

Callum didn't answer. Hunching
his shoulders, he crossed the yard and
disappeared into the farmhouse.

Lorna stared after him, feeling puzzled
and hurt. "What's wrong with him?" she
asked Ruth.

"You know what boys are like,"

Ruth said, rolling her eyes. "You can't say anything to them without getting your head bitten off."

"Most boys. But Callum's not usually like—" Lorna began.

"Stop talking about him, okay?" Ruth broke in, and then she bit her lip. "Sorry. I . . . I didn't mean to yell."

"That's okay," Lorna said quietly.

"I think I'll go up to my room. Mom made up the spare bed for you in there. Are you coming?" Ruth asked.

"I'll come in a minute," Lorna said, still feeling a little confused. Both of her cousins were acting really weird. She waited until Ruth went inside and then sighed as she followed her.

As she trudged past the outbuildings, a flash of bright light suddenly lit up the

workshop windows. Lorna stopped,
shocked. *Strange,* she thought. *I'm sure the
workshop was empty.* She reached out to
give the door a push. "Hello? Is someone
there?"

As the door swung open, revealing
the darkened room, Lorna saw the
outline of what looked to be a tiny toy
kitten sitting on a basket of yarn. In
the dimness, it glowed as if its fur and

whiskers were dotted with a thousand tiny sparkling diamonds.

The fluffy toy must be her aunt's lucky charm. Lorna wondered how she had missed seeing it earlier. "Aren't you gorgeous? You look as if you're really alive," she exclaimed.

The kitten looked up at Lorna with bright green eyes that shone in the dark. "I am alive. Please, can you help me?" it mewed.

Chapter
TWO

Lorna gasped with shock as she
fumbled for the light switch. She could
have sworn that the toy kitten had just
spoken to her!

In the dim light, Lorna could see that
the kitten had fluffy amber-and-white
fur, with an amber patch over one eye, a
bright pink nose, and the biggest emerald
eyes she had ever seen.

It did look very realistic. She moved forward for a closer look. But just as she did, the kitten raised its tiny head.

"I am Prince Flame, heir to the Lion Throne. Who are you?" it meowed inquisitively.

"You really did just speak!" Lorna spluttered. "I'm . . . um, Lorna Edwards. I'm . . . staying here on Craggen Island with my cousins for summer vacation." She was finding it difficult to take this in.

Talking animals only existed in fairy tales—they didn't just turn up in real life! Bending down, she tried to make herself seem smaller, so the amazing kitten wouldn't run away.

"Did you say you're a prince?" she asked him.

Flame nodded, his green eyes gleaming with anger. "But my uncle Ebony has stolen my throne and rules in my place. One day I will return to challenge him and regain my throne!"

"You're a little small for that. If I were you, I'd wait until I grew up," Lorna advised gently.

Flame didn't reply, but instead Lorna saw silver sparks beginning to glitter in Flame's fluffy fur. He sprang off the basket of yarn, and before Lorna could move, she was blinded by another bright silver flash that filled the room.

"Oh!" Lorna rubbed her eyes. When she looked again, she saw that the tiny kitten had disappeared, and in its place stood a magnificent young pure-white lion.

Lorna caught her breath, eyeing the huge paws and sharp teeth. "Flame?"

"Do not be afraid. I will not harm you," the lion told her in a deep velvety roar. There was a final dazzling flash of light, and Flame magically reappeared before her as a tiny amber-and-white kitten, with an amber patch over one eye.

"Wow! That's an amazing disguise. No one would guess that you're a lion prince!" Lorna exclaimed.

"I must hide from my uncle's spies

now. Can you help me, Lorna?" the tiny kitten mewed, trembling from head to toe.

"Of course I will!" Lorna said, picking him up. Flame was impressive as his real lion self, but in his helpless kitten disguise, he was just adorable. "Come on. Let's go into the farmhouse. You're going to love meeting all the family."

"No!" Flame twisted around and gazed up at her. "You can tell no one that I am a prince. It must be our secret!"

Lorna felt a little disappointed that she couldn't even tell Ruth about Flame, but she sighed as she thought sadly that both her cousins didn't seem that delighted to see her, anyway. Lorna felt determined to do whatever Flame wanted to keep him safe. "Okay. Don't worry, I won't give anything away. I'll just say you're a stray or something."

Flame relaxed and blinked up at her with narrowed, trusting eyes. "Thank you, Lorna."

"That's all right. Let's go and find you something to eat. I bet you're hungry," she said.

Flame purred eagerly.

As Lorna crossed the yard, she smiled. Her vacation had just taken an amazingly unexpected turn!

"What a cute little kitten—and I really like his name," Aunt Marie said when Lorna had finished introducing Flame. "He must have smelled the farm cats and come looking for food. We've had a few other strays turn up out of the blue."

"Yes, that's what must have happened,"
Lorna said, glad that she didn't have to go
into more detail about finding Flame. "I
promised him . . . um, I mean, I promised
myself . . . ," she corrected quickly, "that
I'd look after him. Is it okay if I keep
him?" she asked in her best pleading voice.

"Now, Lorna . . . ," her mom said
warningly.

Uncle Hugh laughed. "It's fine with

us, isn't it, Marie?" he said, turning toward his wife. "One more cat won't make much difference, and I don't expect this little fellow will eat much!"

"Only if you're sure . . . ," Lorna's mom said, looking at Marie.

Aunt Marie smiled in agreement. "There's cat food in the barn and some old blankets you can use for Flame's bed."

"Thanks!" Lorna beamed at her aunt and uncle. "I'll feed Flame and then make him a bed in Ruth's room. Come on, Flame!" she called, going outside quickly before anyone could object. There was no way she was going to let her tiny new friend sleep in a drafty old barn!

Lorna slept well and woke to find bright sunlight pushing through a pair of unfamiliar blue curtains. It was a moment before she remembered that she was in the spare bed in Ruth's bedroom with Flame's tiny warm body curled up beside her.

"Hello, you," she whispered, stroking his soft ears. "Did you sleep well?"

"Yes, thank you. I feel safe here with you," Flame purred softly.

Ruth's bed was empty, and Lorna assumed that her cousin had already gone downstairs. She jumped out of bed. "Let's go and get some breakfast," she said to Flame.

Halfway down the stairs, with Flame at her heels, Lorna heard raised voices. She paused and Flame stopped beside her.

"Aw, do I have to come, too, Dad?"
Callum was complaining. "It's so boring.
Anyway, I made plans to meet my friends."

"I'm afraid you'll have to meet them
later," Hugh replied firmly. "You knew I'd
need your help. Besides, I thought you'd
want to spend some time with Lorna.
You've hardly said two words to her since
she arrived."

"Okay then, if I have to," Callum
grumbled.

Lorna heard the bathroom door close, and then Ruth came down the stairs behind her. "What are you waiting here for?" she asked.

"Nothing," Lorna said quickly, feeling a little guilty for eavesdropping.

She, Flame, and Ruth went into the kitchen. Callum was sitting with his chin propped on his hand, slowly stirring a spoon around in a bowl of oatmeal.

"Hi, Callum," Lorna said.

Callum grunted a reply.

"Hello, girls. Help yourselves to oatmeal," Hugh said cheerfully, waving his spoon toward the steaming pot on the stove. "Eat up. We'll have to get going soon."

"Where are we going, Uncle Hugh?" Lorna asked as she fed Flame, before spooning creamy oatmeal into a bowl.

"We're driving to one of the coves. I have to do a beach clean-up and litter survey," Hugh replied.

"Dad's just been made a part-time warden for the nature reserve," Ruth said proudly.

"Big deal," Callum said under his breath.

Hugh grinned patiently. "Cheer up, son! I know picking up litter isn't very exciting, but with a bit of luck, we'll see some seals with their pups."

"Seal pups? Wow!" Lorna didn't care if she had to pick up litter all day, if it meant she got to see some seals. She couldn't wait to see what Flame would make of them.

Chapter
THREE

"Bye! See you later!" Lorna called to her parents and her aunt, who were staying behind at the farm. She picked Flame up before getting into Hugh's Land Rover.

Flame sat on Lorna's lap for the short drive to the cove. Lorna stroked his soft ears as he peered out at the cliffs and the sun sparkling on the blue sea.

Once they were all standing on the white sand of the little cove, Hugh handed out black plastic bags and protective gloves. "Just throw any litter inside. Cans, plastic bags, pieces of old beach balls, whatever. Then we'll list everything you've collected when we meet back here in an hour or so," he instructed.

"Okay, Dad," Ruth said. "Come on, Lorna. Let's do our collecting together."

As Lorna and Ruth headed toward
the shore, Hugh and Callum went off
toward the cliffs. Lorna could see that
her cousin's shoulders were hunched,
and he was dragging his feet. "Looks
like Callum would rather be ten
million miles away!" she said, frowning.

Ruth glared at her brother. "Or
fishing with his new *best* friends!" She
stomped on a discarded paper cup until
it was as flat as a pancake and then
stuffed it into her sack. Turning her
back, she moved away up the beach
and began picking up litter.

Lorna stared after her, blinking in
surprise. "I thought we were supposed
to be doing this together," she
whispered to Flame. "Ruth's as bad as
Callum! One minute she's all friendly,

and then she's so mad! I don't get it."

Flame's furry brow crinkled in a frown. "Perhaps you could ask her what is wrong when she is in a better mood."

Lorna nodded. "Good idea, Flame. I'll do that. Come on, let's collect litter."

The tiny kitten pawed at shells and pebbles, scooting sideways and play growling. Lorna laughed at his antics and soon forgot about her two unpredictable cousins. As she gradually filled the bag, Lorna found that she'd moved closer to a big cluster of rocks at the shore.

One of the small grayish rocks was half submerged in the sea. But to Lorna's surprise, it suddenly moved. It wasn't a rock. It was a baby seal!

"Look over here, Flame!" she whispered, slowly moving closer. Flame padded after her, his ears pricked expectantly.

"Oh no," Lorna gasped in dismay as she spotted the tough fishing line that was tangled around the seal pup's flippers and tail. "The poor little thing. It looks exhausted. I bet it's been trying to get free for ages."

Flame gave a mew of sympathy.

The pup struggled weakly, looking up at her with big helpless dark eyes. Its head drooped and it flopped back down onto the wet sand.

"Don't worry. I'm going to help you," Lorna crooned. She went over to the pup, bent down, and began gently trying to untangle the fishing line.

Then from out of the corner of
her eye she caught a sudden movement
as an enormous seal appeared from
behind the rocks. Baring its strong teeth
and barking with rage, it came toward
Lorna.

The mother seal! It thought Lorna
was trying to hurt its baby.

"It's okay. I'm just . . . just trying to
help." Lorna gulped, edging backward.
Her foot struck a small half-buried rock,
and she fell backward onto the damp
sand.

The mother seal rolled her dark
eyes and hissed with fury. As she lunged
forward, ready to attack, Lorna bit back
a scream.

Time seemed to stand still. But then
a warm tingle flowed down Lorna's

spine. Huge silver sparks began to glow
again in Flame's soft fur. The kitten lifted
a tiny amber, white-tipped paw, and a
bright stream of sparks shot out from
it, raining down gently on the enraged
mother seal and her baby.

The mother seal stopped abruptly
and seemed to calm down. Lorna looked
on in surprise as, with a loud whipping
noise, the tangled fishing line instantly
began to unravel all by itself. In a few

seconds, the pup's flippers and tail were
free, and the fishing line lay in a tangled
heap on the sand. The pup shook itself and
then began slithering toward the sea.

The mother seal took a last long look
at Lorna and then followed her baby.

Lorna got up, her heart still beating
fast. She brushed wet sand from her jeans

as she watched the seals move into
deeper water and then swim away
together. She was happy they were both
okay, even though she still felt shocked
by what had just happened.

She turned to Flame. "Phew!
Thanks for saving me! That was *way* too
close."

"You are welcome," Flame mewed.

Just as the very last spark faded from
Flame's amber-and-white fur, Hugh,
Callum, and Ruth came dashing around
the rocks. "Are you all right?" Uncle
Hugh cried, white-faced. "I heard a
seal's distress cry, then saw a mother
and her pup swimming away! What
happened?"

"I'm fine." Lorna told her uncle
about finding the baby seal, but played

down the part about the mother seal.
"I . . . um, managed to untangle the
fishing line and pull it off," she said,
fibbing a little.

Hugh frowned. "Thank goodness for
that! You seem to have done a good job,
but don't ever, ever try anything like that
by yourself again. You should have called
to me for help. Mother seals can be very
dangerous when they're protecting their
young! She could have attacked you."

Tell me about it, Lorna thought; her
heartbeat was only now returning to
normal.

Ruth looked at Lorna admiringly.
"Wow! You were brave."

"Not really. I was scared to death!"
Lorna admitted.

Even Callum looked impressed. "Way

to go, Lorna," he said, giving her a big grin.

Lorna grinned back. It was the first time since she'd arrived that Callum seemed like his old self.

Hugh picked up the broken fishing line. "I wish the idiots who leave this stuff around could see what harm it causes. Most fishermen are responsible, but the few who aren't ruin it for the others . . ."

"Do you need me anymore, Dad?" Callum broke in impatiently. "I'm supposed to be meeting my friends, remember?"

"What?" Hugh looked at his son. "All right. I suppose I can manage without you now. Where are you going?"

"Just to a classmate's house. See you

later, everyone!" Callum called, already
jogging toward a path that led inland from
the beach.

"Callum!" Ruth called after her
brother, but he didn't turn around. Only
Lorna saw the worried look on Ruth's
face, which she quickly changed to a smile
as she turned back toward her dad.

Chapter
FOUR

Lorna and Ruth finished helping
Hugh list all the beach litter for the survey.
It seemed to take forever, and Lorna was
glad when they were finally putting the
clipboards, pens, and bags of litter into her
uncle's car.

"Thank you very much, girls—and
kitten," Hugh said, bending down to
stroke Flame's fluffy amber-and-white fur.

"I think you all deserve a treat after your hard work. How does hot chocolate with extra whipped cream sound? Come on. We'll go to the café in town!"

"Yes!" Lorna and Ruth chorused. Flame gave an eager mew.

Hugh laughed. "Sounds like Flame's looking forward to a saucer of cream!

I reckon that little kitten understands everything we say."

Lorna smiled to herself. If only Uncle Hugh knew!

It was a short drive to the stores in town. On the way, Hugh discovered a grocery list in his pocket. "Oh! I just remembered that I promised to bring some things back for Marie. I just need to pop into the supermarket." He pulled into the parking lot and parked the car. "This won't take long. You may as well wait in the car, and then we'll go straight to the café."

"Okay, Dad," Ruth said.

Lorna sat in the back of the Land Rover with Flame on her lap as Hugh disappeared into the supermarket. She glanced around idly and noticed some boys messing around near a row of shopping carts. One of them looked familiar.

"That looks like Callum over there," she said.

"Where?" Ruth turned her head. "It *is* him! I knew he wasn't going to his classmate's house. He's with those older boys again. The one with the black hair is called Sam and the one with a round face and freckles is Larry."

"You don't seem to like them very much," Lorna said.

"I don't!" Ruth said. "Sam and Larry are always getting into trouble. Mom and Dad don't know that Callum hangs out with them."

Things started to fall into place for Lorna. "But you knew, didn't you?"

Ruth nodded unhappily. "I found out when I saw Callum with them at the park."

"Maybe you should tell your mom and dad what's going on," Lorna suggested.

"I'm not a tattletale!" Ruth said indignantly, glancing over at the three boys again. "But if Dad sees them together, he'll go nuts. I have to warn Callum to stay out of sight." She got out of the car and started hurrying over to the shopping carts.

"Come on, Flame. Let's follow her!" Lorna said, setting Flame down on the ground. As she ran after Ruth, he scampered along at her heels. Lorna saw Sam climbing into a shopping cart, and then Callum and Larry began dragging it around in circles.

"Hey!" Ruth called. As she almost reached the boys, they gave the shopping cart an extra-big shove and let it go.

It zoomed past Ruth and hurtled straight at Lorna and Flame. Lorna quickly stepped sideways, but Flame's tiny legs couldn't move fast enough. The heavy cart veered toward him, wheels rattling. He was about to be run over!

"Flame! Look out!" Lorna cried. She knew he couldn't use his magic without giving himself away.

Throwing herself forward, she reached desperately for the shopping cart. Her fingers brushed against the metal side and then just managed to grab hold of it. The cart swung sideways, wrenching her arm painfully and

missing Flame by a whisker, before it
rolled away across the parking lot.

"Ow!" Lorna cried out as a hot wave
of pain shot up her arm.

But Flame was safe. He bounded up
to her and twined himself around her
ankles. "Thank you, Lorna," he purred
softly. "But I am sorry that you were hurt
when you were saving me."

"I'll be okay," Lorna whispered
bravely, although she could almost feel

the color draining out of her face. "I'd hate it if anything happened to you."

The cart had stopped now and Sam climbed out. "What did you grab it for? It almost tipped over!" he shouted at Lorna.

Callum came running over with Larry at his side. "What are you doing here, anyway? Are you spying on me, you nosy little brat?" Callum hissed at Ruth.

Despite her sore arm, Lorna felt her temper rising. "Oh, shut up, Callum! Ruth didn't even know you were here! Uncle Hugh just stopped by to go shopping. But you and your stupid friends almost ran Flame over!" she stormed.

Sam's eyes narrowed, and he took a step toward Lorna. "What did you just call us?"

"It's okay, Sam. She's my cousin," Callum said hastily. He turned to Lorna. "You shouldn't have interfered. It's your fault if that kitten got in the way!"

"For goodness' sake, Callum! Can't you see that Lorna's hurt her arm?" Ruth shouted, almost in tears.

Callum's face straightened. "I didn't realize. Sorry, Lorna. Is it bad?"

Sam and Larry exchanged sly looks. "Gotta go!" Sam said.

"Me too! Let's get out of here!" Larry said.

"Typical!" Ruth said to Callum as both boys ran away. "I don't think much of your special new friends!" She turned to Lorna. "Let's go and find Dad. He'll know what to do."

Lorna's arm was aching so much now

that she didn't argue. She scooped Flame
up with her good arm and held him
against her side as she followed Ruth.

Callum stood there, undecided.

"There's no point in me coming with
you. I can't do anything. What are you
going to tell Dad?"

"I don't know yet," Ruth called back.
"Shouldn't you go after Sam and Larry

before he sees you?"

"Ruth . . . ," Callum began, but then he stopped and his face took on the grumpy expression that Lorna was getting used to seeing. "I hope your arm's okay," Callum said quickly to her, before turning and going after his friends.

"If you can find somewhere where we can be alone, I will make your arm better," Flame purred softly to Lorna.

Lorna nodded, wincing. As they went inside the supermarket, she spotted the ladies' bathroom. "I'm just going to pop in here," she said to Ruth.

"Should I come in with you?" Ruth asked.

Lorna shook her head. "No. I'll be fine."

"All right. I'll wait outside," Ruth said.

Luckily there was no one else in the
bathroom. As Lorna closed the door,
big silver sparks were already igniting
in Flame's amber-and-white fur, and
his whiskers crackled with electricity.
He lifted a tiny paw and sent a spray of
twinkling glitter toward Lorna's sore
arm. It showered gently onto her, and

immediately her arm felt all warm and tingly. The pain increased for a second and then it seemed to drain down her arm and flow right out of the ends of her fingers.

"Wow! Thanks, Flame. My arm feels fine now," she said. She gave him an affectionate cuddle, and he licked her chin with his rough little tongue. A few seconds later she emerged from the bathroom carrying Flame in both arms.

Ruth gave her a puzzled look. "Your arm seems a lot better."

"It's absolutely fine now. I, er . . . splashed cold water on it," Lorna said. "Mom did that when I hit my knee once. It worked great. No need to say anything to Uncle Hugh."

"Hello, you two. Did you get bored

waiting for me?" Hugh came toward them, holding plastic bags of groceries.

"Yes, we did," Lorna said, smiling brightly. "Can we go to the café now, please?"

Chapter
FIVE

"Dad has to go across to one of the smaller islands today. We're all going with him and taking a picnic lunch," Ruth said the following day.

"Sounds great!" Lorna said. "Is Callum coming, too?"

Ruth nodded. "He's been on his best behavior since yesterday. I think he's still worried that I'll tell Dad about what happened in the parking lot."

"Are you going to?" Lorna asked.

"No!" Ruth shook her head, grinning. "But don't tell Callum!"

They both laughed.

Lorna went to fetch her shoulder bag. She put the bag onto the floor so that Flame could jump inside before they all walked down to the small jetty, which was just past the garden.

As Lorna climbed into *Seagull*, Hugh's small but powerful motorboat, the sea breeze ruffled her short red hair. She shaded her eyes with her hand, looking at the humped shapes of the islands across the narrow channel.

Callum stood waiting until everyone except Hugh was on board. "Can I go across in the dinghy instead of coming with you, Dad?"

Hugh thought about it and then shook his head. "It's not safe today. There's a chance of storms and high tides. I'd rather we all went in *Seagull*."

"Aw, Da-ad. I've been over to the islands in the dinghy lots of times. I'm a strong rower," Callum grumbled.

Hugh gave him a level look. "I'm not going to argue with you, Callum."

Sighing heavily, Callum got on board
Seagull and flopped down next to Lorna.
Hugh got into the cabin and started the
engine, and the boat moved away from the
jetty.

Flame sat on Lorna's lap, his nose in
the air as he sniffed the sea breeze. The
waves slapped against the boat, and Lorna
tasted salty spray on her lips.

In only a few minutes they were
drawing level with some sandbanks.
Dozens of mother seals and their pups
were dotted all over them.

"I wonder if the pup we . . . er, I mean
I, untangled is over there with its mom,"
Lorna said. She felt Flame nudge her hand
as she corrected herself in front of the
others.

"The pups only stay with their

mothers for a couple of weeks. Then they're off to fend for themselves," Hugh told Lorna. He slowed *Seagull*'s engine so everyone could have a good look at the seals before then steering the boat toward the island.

Once *Seagull* was moored, everyone got out and trudged up the beach with the picnic things.

As Lorna helped spread out a picnic blanket, hundreds of gulls and fulmars wheeled overhead and puffins flapped inland, their yellow beaks stuffed with sand eels. Flame craned his neck, looking up at all the birds excitedly, and almost tripped over his own paws.

Lorna hid a smile. Sometimes it was hard to remember that Flame was a royal prince!

Lunch was delicious. Aunt Marie had even remembered to put in a little packet of dry cat food. Flame munched it happily. Afterward Ruth, Callum, Lorna, and Flame went with Hugh to check out the ledges and cliffs for nesting birds. Lorna put Flame back inside her shoulder bag as they clambered over some extra-big rocks at the base of the cliffs.

As she climbed down the steep rocks onto a stretch of beach, Lorna spotted a brightly colored dinghy on the pebbled part of the shore. Two boys were sitting nearby, fishing.

"See that dinghy? I *said* it would be okay to row over here," Callum said pointedly to his dad.

Hugh ignored him and strode over to the boys. "Hey, you there! Do you realize

this is a nature reserve? I hope you have
fishing permits," he called.

The boys stood up and turned around.
Lorna recognized them now. It was Sam
and Larry. Catching sight of Callum, the
older boys waved.

Callum looked sheepish and pretended
not to notice. He kicked at some sand
with one sneaker and then turned his
back.

Hugh gave Callum a sharp look and

then turned to Sam and Larry. "Hello, boys. What are you up to?"

"Just fishing, Mr. Neel," Sam said politely. "We usually fish over on the other side of the island. We didn't know we had to have permits for here."

"Yeah, sorry about that. But we haven't actually caught anything yet," Larry said glumly.

"Fish not biting, huh?" Hugh said. His face softened slightly. "Well, you don't seem to be doing any harm. I'll forget about the permit, just this once. Make sure you keep away from any nests and young birds and clean up after yourselves, all right? We've had some problems with broken fishing line being left around."

"Well, it wasn't ours. We always take

our trash home," Sam said indignantly.

"Glad to hear it. And be careful in
that dinghy when you go back, boys.
A storm can blow up quickly on that
narrow stretch," Hugh advised as he
walked away.

"We will!" Sam and Larry chorused.
"Thanks, Mr. Neel."

"Just listen to Dad, giving orders!"
Callum muttered, red-faced. "Why
does he have to be *so* embarrassing?"
Clenching his fists, he stomped back
across the dunes toward their picnic site.

Ruth frowned as she watched her
brother go.

Later that afternoon, back from their
trip on *Seagull*, Lorna, Flame, and Ruth
searched for unusual shells. Hugh had

gone off to check another area of the
reserve, Callum was nowhere in sight, and
Lorna's mom, dad, and aunt were on the
beach, reading and sunbathing.

"Look at this one!" Lorna exclaimed,
bending down to pick up a large pebble.
"It looks just like a curled-up sleeping
kitten!"

"Oh yes," Ruth agreed. "It reminds
me of Flame. Look, it's even got amber-
and-white marks on it."

To her delight, Lorna saw that Ruth
was right. She slipped the pebble into her
jeans pocket. After another ten minutes,
she pushed a lock of damp red hair off
her forehead. "I'm really hot now. Let's
go for a paddle in this rock pool," she
suggested.

Ruth nodded. "Great idea!"

Flame sat on a rock as Ruth and
Lorna rolled up their jeans, took off
their shoes and socks, and padded over
to the pool. "Phew! This stuff is smelly,"
Lorna said as her foot squished in some
seaweed.

Ruth wrinkled her nose. "You're not
kidding!"

Once in the water, they forgot about
the smelly seaweed. They sloshed around,
enjoying themselves. Neither of them
noticed Callum, Sam, and Larry creeping
up on them.

"Got them!" called a triumphant
voice.

Lorna whipped around to see Sam
waving their shoes and socks in the
air. "Very funny. Give them back!" she
demanded.

Sam threw one shoe across to Larry, who caught it and grinned. "If you want them back, you'll have to come and get them!"

Lorna put her hands on her hips. She knew just where this was going to end up, and it was too hot to chase the boys all over the beach as they threw the shoes and socks to each other. "Oh, why don't you grow up!" she shouted crossly.

Sam's eyebrows drew together in a scowl. "I've had just about enough of that snotty kid! I don't care if she is your cousin!" he grumbled to Callum. Lifting his arm, he went to throw the shoes and socks into the pool.

Lorna felt a familiar warm tingling down her back. *Now you've really done it, Sam,* she thought.

She heard a faint crackle of sparks from behind a nearby rock. With a whooshing sound, a sharp breeze lifted all the stinking seaweed into the air. The whole slimy mess shot toward Sam and splattered onto his head and shoulders.

"Argh! Mnnff!" Sam gave a muffled cry. Dropping the shoes, he stumbled around, clawing the seaweed off.

"He looks like that shaggy old mop Mom uses on the floor!" Ruth said, giggling.

"Look out, Sam!" Callum shouted, but it was too late.

There was a huge splash as Sam toppled into the pool right next to Lorna and Ruth, soaking them both. Moments later, he jumped up, furiously spitting out water. Despite being soaked,

Lorna and Ruth fell over laughing, and even Larry and Callum were biting back grins.

"That was a freaky breeze! I've never seen it lift up seaweed like that before," Ruth said when she could speak again.

"Mmm," Lorna agreed. She winked at Flame as he jumped out from behind the rock and stood there twitching his tail. "That'll teach those mean boys to mess with us!" she whispered to him while everyone was still looking at Sam.

Chapter
SIX

Over the next few days, the weather was dull and rainy, but the big storm that everyone had been expecting seemed to have passed by Craggen.

At first, Lorna didn't mind it being gloomy. It was fun exploring the local market with her cousins. Even sheltering under an umbrella was okay with Flame tucked under her arm.

Another day, Lorna's parents drove them all to the ferry, and they went to the indoor roller rink on the mainland.

"This is great, isn't it?" Lorna whispered over her shoulder to Flame as she zoomed back and forth on her Rollerblades.

Flame was peering up out of her backpack, his front paws clinging on tight and his eyes bright with excitement.

"I like it when we go really fast!" he mewed happily.

But by the third day, when an angry gray sky hung over the farm and surrounding hills, Lorna found herself longing for sunny weather. "I'm sick of shopping, and we can't go to the beach. What should we do?" she asked, glancing at the rain running down the living-room window.

Ruth thought hard. "How about watching TV? Or I could get out my old Barbie dolls?"

"TV or dolls?" Callum said disgustedly, just coming into the room. "I'd rather eat my own leg! Wait here, you two."

Lorna smiled to herself. Callum had been great for the last few days, away from Sam and Larry, and now it looked like he might be having one of his brainstorms.

Callum reappeared minutes later
with an atlas of the world, a pen and
paper, and his dad's stopwatch. Lorna and
Ruth waited, intrigued.

"Okay. This game is called Race the
World," Callum explained, spreading
open the atlas. "It works like this. We all
make a list of towns from the index. It's
fun if you can find really weird-sounding

ones. And then we take turns searching for them."

"What's the watch for?" Ruth wanted to know.

"Everyone gets five minutes to find as many towns as they can. That's why it's called a race. Whoever finds the most towns by the end of the game gets this!" He held up a bag of lemon drops.

Lorna's mouth watered. "Sounds great," she said eagerly. "Can I have the first turn at making a list of towns for you two to find?"

"Okay," Ruth and Callum agreed.

Flame folded his front paws beneath him as he watched from the sofa.

It was very fun, finding really weird-sounding towns and then racing to find them in the atlas. Lorna and her cousins

were soon squealing with laughter.
An hour passed by, unnoticed. It was
Lorna's third turn. She was about to
turn a page, when suddenly a tiny fluffy
shape leaped onto the atlas. "Watch
out, Flame! You're in the middle of the
Pacific Ocean!" she said, spluttering
with laughter.

As Flame blinked at her with big
innocent green eyes and then began
washing himself, Ruth started giggling.
"I think that's Flame's way of saying
that he's bored!"

Callum grinned and reached over
to stroke Flame's fluffy fur. "Okay. Have
it your way, Flame. Game's over. I vote
we share the candy."

"Fine with us!" chorused Lorna and
Ruth.

They were all munching lemon drops when the phone rang in the hall. Lorna heard her uncle pick it up and start speaking. His voice sounded serious.

"Uh-oh, sounds like trouble," said Ruth to the others.

When Hugh came into the living room a couple of minutes later, he wore a serious expression. "That was the local police. Someone reported seeing smoke coming from the reserve on Seal Island. They went to investigate and found Sam and Larry. They'd lit a fire and had been pouring all kinds of stuff on it to keep it going." Hugh shook his head. "I can't believe they were so stupid. And after I let them off about the fishing permit."

"Sam and Larry are okay. They were just messing around," Callum said. "It's no big deal."

"I'm afraid I can't agree with you," his father replied soberly. "Who knows what would have happened if it had been a hot day? Fire can easily get out of control and cause terrible damage to

wildlife. Besides, Sam and Larry could
have burned themselves badly. I'm sorry,
Callum. Those boys are trouble. I want
you to stay away from them."

"But Da-ad! We were going night
fishing tomorrow . . . ," Callum burst
out and then stopped guiltily as he saw
Hugh's set look. "I was going to tell you
about it, honest! I can still go, can't I?"

Lorna couldn't help feeling sorry for
her older cousin. It was clear that Uncle
Hugh wasn't going to change his mind.

Callum had realized that, too. "You
never want me to have any fun, do
you?" he shouted tearfully at his father
before storming out. Ruth ran upstairs
after her brother, but Lorna heard the
bathroom door slam.

"Poor Callum. I hope he's okay,"

she said to Flame as she cleaned up
the remnants of their Race the World
game.

Flame nodded sympathetically.
"Perhaps it is best if he stays away from
the older boys."

Lorna remembered how Sam and
Larry had almost run Flame over with
the shopping cart, and she had to
agree.

That evening, Lorna and Ruth
were sitting in Ruth's bedroom
listening to music. Lorna was holding
the pebble shaped like a curled-up
kitten and running her fingers over it.

Callum appeared in the open
doorway. He glared straight at Lorna.
"You put Dad up to this, didn't you?"

Lorna gaped at him. "What do you mean?" she asked, puzzled.

"I've been thinking about it. You must have blabbed about what happened in the parking lot. That's why Dad went ballistic at me. It couldn't have been just 'cause of Sam and Larry lighting fires!"

Ruth rushed to Lorna's defense.
"Stop it, Callum. Lorna doesn't tattle; she
wouldn't!"

"Huh! And I'm supposed to believe
that?" Callum sneered.

Lorna swallowed. She knew that
Callum was angry and upset, but he
didn't have to take it out on her. "You can
believe what you like! You're just trying to
find excuses for your horrible friends. It's
Sam and Larry you want to pick a fight
with, not me!" she said furiously.

Callum looked at her closely and
seemed to be satisfied. "Whatever! Anyway,
I don't care what anyone says, I *am* going
night fishing with Sam and Larry, so
there!" He turned away.

Moments later, Lorna and Ruth heard
his bedroom door slam.

"Do you think he meant it about going night fishing?" Ruth asked worriedly.

"No. He's just whining. He wouldn't dare, not after what Uncle Hugh said." But in her heart she wasn't so certain. She'd never seen Callum so upset.

Chapter
SEVEN

The following day, Aunt Marie had to take some of her woven blankets to a store on the mainland. Lorna, Flame, and Ruth went with Marie, while Lorna's parents went off to shop for some local treats.

Uncle Hugh was working on the farm, and Callum was helping him. After delivering the blankets, Aunt Marie took

Lorna, Flame, and Ruth to the movies. "I
think we should leave Flame in the car.
He might be scared by the loud noises,"
she suggested.

Lorna looked down at Flame, who
was curled up in her lap in the backseat.
She saw him give a slight shake of his
head. "I think he'll be fine, Auntie. I can
always bring him back out if he seems
upset," she said.

"All right, dear. I'll leave it up to
you," Aunt Marie said, smiling.

In the movie theater, Flame seemed spellbound by the big screen with its larger-than-life actors and bright colors. The film was an exciting sci-fi adventure. Lorna smiled as Flame twitched his ears and put his head to one side, enjoying the amazing special effects.

She wondered if he'd been to the movies before. Perhaps this wasn't the only time he'd visited this world. Lorna felt a flicker of pride that Flame had chosen her for his friend.

After the movie, they met up again with Lorna's parents. As Aunt Marie drove back across Craggen, dark clouds hung low over the mountains. "Looks like there's still a chance of us having a storm," she commented. "I'd better make sure the animals are all safe tonight."

When they arrived at the farmhouse, Callum and Uncle Hugh still were out checking on the sheep.

"Can me and Lorna help make supper, Mom?" Ruth asked.

Marie smiled. "What did you have in mind?"

"Cheese-and-potato pie?" Lorna suggested. Her mom had shown her how to make it.

"Sounds good. Let's see what I've got to go with it," her aunt replied.

Lorna and Ruth tied on aprons and got to work. Lorna didn't notice Flame glancing warily over his shoulder before slinking out of the kitchen and running upstairs.

Just as supper was ready, Hugh and

Callum appeared.

"Something smells good. I'm starving," Hugh said.

"Me too," Callum agreed.

"It's cheese-and-potato pie, with sausages and beans. Ruth and I made it," Lorna said.

Hugh made a face. "I think I just lost my appetite."

"Hey!" Lorna said, grinning and nudging her uncle in the ribs.

Supper was a great success, and Lorna saved a small dishful for Flame, who hadn't appeared for dinner. She felt happy and relaxed. Callum was his funny, playful self and even told one of his terrible jokes. That evening, they all played Callum's Race the World game. This time they played in teams. Hugh tried to cheat, but he was so bad at it that everyone noticed. Lorna laughed so much her stomach ached.

By the time she went up to bed, Lorna was tired but relaxed. She was really glad that Callum seemed to have made up with his dad and forgotten all about going night fishing.

She saw the tip of Flame's tail sticking out from under her pillow. "You must be extra sleepy to have missed dinner," she

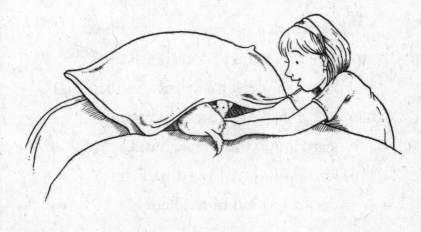

teased, slipping her hands beneath it
to pick him up, but he shied away. She
frowned. He'd never done that before.

Her face dropped as she realized that
the tiny kitten was trembling all over.
"What's wrong? Are you sick?"

Flame flattened his ears and crawled
beneath the comforter. "My enemies are
near. If I stay quiet and still, they may
pass me by," he told her in a muffled
little whine.

Lorna woke up with a start. She sat
up, staring into the darkness of Ruth's
bedroom, wondering what it was that
had woken her. She listened carefully
and heard a dull thudding sound.

Her first thought was that Flame's
enemies had found him. She felt a

flicker of alarm for him, and her heart
missed a beat, but then she felt the
kitten's warm little body move close to
her. A wave of relief flowed over her.
Flame hadn't needed to leave, so he must
be safe for now.

"Can you hear that thudding?" she
whispered to him.

"Yes. It sounds like a door banging,"
Flame mewed softly, jumping off the
bed.

Lorna frowned, her heart beating
fast. She slipped out of bed after him,
crept out of the bedroom, and went
slowly downstairs. The farmhouse was
creepy in the darkness, but she didn't feel
frightened as long as Flame was padding
along beside her.

As Lorna went into the kitchen and

turned on the light, she saw that the door
to the back porch was open. As each gust
of wind hit it, it banged back and forth on
its old-fashioned latch.

"That's weird. I know Aunt Marie was
really careful to lock up—" she began,
when suddenly a jagged flash of lightning
lit up the darkened window. A massive
crack of thunder followed immediately.

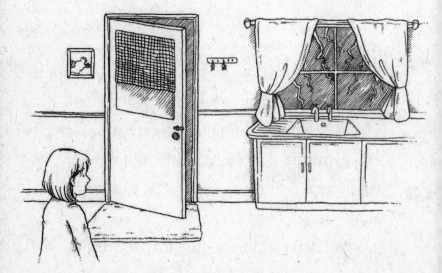

Lorna almost jumped out of her skin.
The storm that had been threatening
for days was finally here. She listened
for any movement from upstairs, but no
one stirred, not even when the thunder
rolled around for a second and third
time. "They must still be asleep. I guess
they're used to storms on Craggen.
And Mom and Dad always say that
they could sleep through the end of the
world!"

Flame's furry brow wrinkled in a
frown, and his hackles stood up. "Perhaps
someone has tried to get in."

Lorna thought that wasn't likely.
The farmhouse was well hidden in the
hills and very hard to find. A dreadful
suspicion shot into her mind. "What
about if someone was going *out*, not

trying to get *in*? Come on!" she hissed to Flame, already racing back upstairs.

"Where are we going?" he mewed curiously, bounding after her.

"To Callum's room!"

Lorna tiptoed quietly across the hall and opened Callum's bedroom door. There was a lumpy shape in his bed. It was okay after all, then. But as she drew closer, she could see that the shape beneath the comforter looked odd.

"Callum?" she whispered, reaching out to shake him gently, but her fingers sank right down into the soft blanket. Throwing it back, she saw the bunched pillow and rolled clothes.

Lorna gasped. "He's gone! And I think I know where—night fishing with Sam and Larry. He's going to be in terrible

trouble. We have to go after him, Flame!"
As if to underline her words, there was
another flash of lightning and a crack of
thunder.

Lorna quickly pulled her jeans and
sweater on over her nightgown.

Downstairs, she grabbed a hooded
raincoat and thrust her feet into rubber
boots. Scooping Flame up, she slipped him
inside the coat and dashed outside.

Rain was lashing down as she splashed
across the farmyard and hurried toward
the small jetty, where *Seagull* was moored.
Another dazzling flash of lightning lit up
the narrow sea channel, and Lorna gasped
with horror.

In that brief glimpse, she had seen a
tiny orange shape battling with the wind
and the waves. There were three people

inside it.

"It's Sam and Larry's dinghy!" she shouted to Flame above the noise of the storm. "They're trying to row across to Seal Island. And Callum's with them!"

Chapter
EIGHT

Lorna's first thought was to dash back to the house and wake everyone up, but that would waste precious time.

The thought of that tiny helpless dinghy on the rough sea made her shudder. "We have to do something— now!" she shouted to Flame above the wind.

Flame nodded. "Follow me!" He

streaked toward *Seagull*, trailing sparks like
a tiny comet. Lorna didn't hesitate. She ran
after the brave kitten and quickly got on
board. Flame scampered straight into the
cabin. Lorna felt a familiar warm tingling
down her spine as the biggest silver sparks
she'd seen yet began glowing in Flame's
fluffy amber-and-white fur.

Leaning forward, Flame opened his mouth wide and puffed out a twinkling fountain of bright blue glitter toward *Seagull*'s control panel. For a moment all the controls and the ship's wheel gleamed in the dark and then looked normal again. To Lorna's astonishment, the boat's powerful engine rumbled to life and all the lights came on.

"I think it would be best if you drove. Fingers are better at turning a wheel," Flame purred, holding up his tiny paws.

"Er . . . okay." Lorna gulped, feeling scared and nervous, but she trusted Flame and knew that he'd never let any harm come to her. "I'll untie the mooring rope."

As soon as she came back into the cabin, Lorna took the wheel, and *Seagull* seemed to slip away from the jetty all by herself. "This is easier than I thought," she said, glancing at Flame, who sat peering out at the choppy, white-capped waves.

Thunder roared and lightning flashed, but *Seagull* powered through the sea,

moving ever closer to the tiny dinghy. *Almost there*, Lorna thought. *Hang on Callum, we're coming!*

As the motorboat drew alongside the dinghy, Lorna saw Flame raise a tiny paw, and then she felt *Seagull*'s engines slow and the boat came to a full stop, staying put exactly as if she had dropped anchor. Lorna dashed out onto the deck. Holding on to the handrail firmly, she leaned over and looked down through the rain. In the dinghy below her, three scared white faces peered up. She saw that all the boys were wearing life jackets.

"Dad, I'm sorry . . . ," Callum began, looking up at the motorboat. "Whoa! Lorna, what—"

"Never mind that now. Quick!

Grab the ladder and climb up," Lorna ordered.

For once, the boys didn't argue. Callum and then Sam climbed aboard *Seagull*. Lorna helped them up and then reached down to Larry. Just as Larry stepped onto the deck, a big wave crashed against the dinghy and flipped it over. A gust of wind then took it and carried it away until it was just a tiny orange dot against the angry sky.

"We could have been in that," Sam gasped, horrified.

"Don't think about it. You're safe now. I'm taking you back to shore," Lorna said. She took the wheel and as the terrified boys gazed out to sea where the dinghy had once been,

Flame magically gunned *Seagull*'s engine
to life. "We've got them, Flame. And it's all
thanks to you!" she whispered.

"You are welcome," Flame purred,
settling close by her as the motorboat
swung around and headed back toward
the jetty.

Sam and Larry huddled together,
shivering under Hugh's spare raincoats.
Callum came and stood next to Lorna

at the wheel. "I n–never . . . knew you could drive a . . . b–boat," he stammered, sounding impressed, even though his teeth were chattering.

"Oh, I'm full of surprises," Lorna said, her eyes gleaming. If only he knew!

"Thank goodness you are, or we'd be in a bigger mess now—or worse. Dad's going to ground me for a year when he hears about this!" Callum said miserably.

"Not if he doesn't find out. Everyone

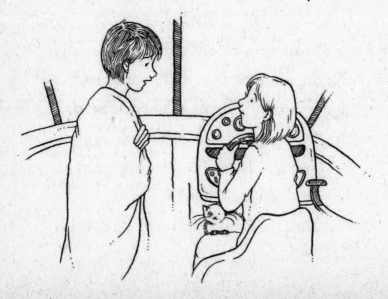

was asleep when I left, despite the storm. I don't think they'd have heard *Seagull*'s engine. If we're lucky, we'll be able to creep back in before they wake up," Lorna said.

"Really? You're amazing, Lorna!" Callum said, beaming at her.

"She's okay for a girl," Sam said quietly.

Lorna grinned. That was probably all the thanks she was going to get!

Seagull reached the jetty safely and glided smoothly to a stop at her mooring. As the engine switched off automatically, Lorna jumped out and tied her up.

"Thanks, Lorna!" Sam and Larry mumbled, before scampering up the jetty and shooting off home.

Callum pulled at her arm impatiently.

"Come on, we'd better hurry. If Mom and Dad wake up and find us gone, we're *both* toast! Flame will follow us."

"Okay, I get the message!" Lorna said. The two of them began jogging toward the garden as quickly and quietly as they could.

Chapter
NINE

To Lorna's relief, there were no lights on at the farmhouse. She, Flame, and Callum quickly slipped inside.

"Who . . . who's there?" Ruth's small, scared voice came out of the darkness of the stairwell.

"It's only me and Lorna!" Callum hissed back. "Hush! You'll wake Mom and Dad."

"I thought it was burglars!" Ruth whispered, coming down the stairs. "Why are you two creeping around?"

Callum grabbed his sister's arm and pulled her into the kitchen. "Come in here and I'll tell you everything!"

Lorna let Callum explain about how she had rescued him, Sam, and

Larry from the dinghy. Ruth listened in amazement, her eyes widening as Callum finished speaking. "I should have known that Sam and Larry had something to do with this!" she said grumpily. "You could have all been drowned. You're a complete idiot, Callum! And Lorna's been fantastic, even though you've been so mean to her."

"I know you're right," Callum said, looking subdued. "Dad tried to warn me, but I was too stubborn to listen. Tonight's changed all that. Sam and Larry are history from now on, as far as I'm concerned." He turned to Lorna. "I'm really sorry I've been such a pain. I'm going to make it up to you by making this the best vacation we've

all had together. You're a completely
amazing cousin."

Lorna blushed hard. "Thanks. That's
okay."

Ruth gave a relieved smile. "Thank
goodness things are back to normal. I
know what we need now."

"What?" Lorna and Callum
chorused in whispers.

"A group hug!"

"Yuck! Do we have to?" Callum
screwed up his face and made pretend
gagging noises. They all hugged while
trying to muffle their giggles.

After they broke apart, Ruth
yawned. "We'd better go back to bed.
Come on, Callum." They trudged out
of the kitchen.

"I'll come up in a minute. I'm just

going to get a drink," Lorna said. She
waited until her cousins had gone
upstairs before bending down to stroke
Flame. "Thanks again for everything.
You've been fantastic tonight," she
whispered.

"I am just happy that I could
still be here to help," Flame purred,
rubbing himself against her hand and
gazing up at her with bright emerald
eyes. Lorna bent down to pick him
up and then laid her cheek against his
silky fur. As she breathed in his sweet
kitten smell, she felt a big surge of
affection for him.

Flame's enemies were still close,
and they wouldn't stop looking for
him. For his own safety, he might
have to leave suddenly. And if that

happened, Lorna knew that she was
going to have to be very brave and let
her magical friend go.

Lorna woke suddenly the following
morning. Pinkish dawn light was just
beginning to creep through the curtains.
She stretched out her hand to stroke
Flame, but there was just a tiny warm
dent in the comforter where he had
been lying.

A cold feeling came over her as a suspicion rose in her mind. She quickly got up and padded downstairs.

"Flame! Where are you?" she whispered, checking the hall and kitchen.

Suddenly a bright silver flash came from the living room. Lorna rushed inside. A magnificent, regal young white lion stood in front of the sofa. She had almost forgotten how impressive and beautiful Flame was as his real self. His white fur glinted with thousands of sparkling points of light.

An older gray lion with a wise, kind face stood next to Flame.

And then Lorna knew for certain that Flame's enemies had found him, and he was leaving for real this time.

"Prince Flame. We must hurry," the old gray lion rumbled.

Lorna felt a deep pang of sadness. "I'll never forget you, Flame!" she said, throwing her arms around Flame's neck.

"You've been a good friend. Be well, Lorna. Stand back now," Prince Flame said in a deep velvety roar.

As Lorna backed away, there was a final flash, and bright silver sparkles whirled around the two lions like a snowstorm, crackling to the carpet at Lorna's feet. And then the two big cats were gone.

Lorna bit back her tears, glad that Flame was safe. At least she'd had the chance to say good-bye to him. "Take care, wherever you go," she whispered.

Her hand brushed against something

in her jeans pocket. As she reached inside, her fingers closed over something cold.

A slow smile spread over Lorna's face as she took out the pebble shaped like a curled-up kitten. It would always be a wonderful reminder of the marvelous magic kitten who had shared her island adventure.

About the Author

Sue Bentley's books for children often include animals or fairies. She lives in Northampton, England, and enjoys reading, going to the movies, and sitting watching the frogs and newts in her garden pond. If she hadn't been a writer, she would probably have been a skydiver or brain surgeon. The main reason she writes is that she can drink pots and pots of tea while she's typing. She has met and owned many cats, and each one has brought a special sort of magic to her life.

Don't miss these Magic Kitten books!